Kissing the Monster Hunter

Meg Pokrass

BAMBOO DART PRESS

LOS ANGELES † NEW YORK † LONDON † MELBOURNE

Kissing the Monster Hunter by Meg Pokrass

978-1-947240-47-6   Paperback
978-1-947240-48-3   eBook

Cover art by Dennis Callaci and Meg Pokrass

Layout and design by Mark Givens

For information:

Bamboo Dart Press

chapbooks@bamboodartpress.com

Bamboo Dart Press 030

www.pelekinesis.com

www.bamboodartpress.com

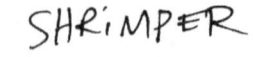
www.shrimperrecords.com

For Gretchen,
who understands the importance of dreams.

CONTENTS

ELOPEMENT ON THE LOCH

The inky black waters of Loch Ness attract the strangest visitors.

You eloped this morning. You are now man and wife—or woman and husband!—popping antihistamines and hoping not to vomit, holding hands on this misty ride on the Caledonia canal, approaching the widening mouth: your fantasy honeymoon quest, to see the loch together.

"Feel that wave?" he says, his skin a bit damp.

"What wave?" you ask, wishing you had felt something. Usually, you feel and he doesn't. You're the one attuned to the submerged shapes that don't exist: Monsters in anything and everything.

You clutch your mother's frayed wedding hat, its gritty original netting.

"You're cute enough to charm the monster," he says with salty lips, spots of rain speckling his shirt. His skin reminds you of childhood, the smell of a surprise waiting to happen, or a promise almost ready to be kept.

Underneath the tourist boat, you imagine, are the bubbles of your mother's failed marriage, a deep loch creature, freshwater sadness in her eyes.

"Look! There's something over there," you say, pointing to the glint of a shadow, the sun shining off something dark and unhappy, a large slimy rock or a tiny island built on bird guano. Or maybe you're just pointing at a distant tourist boat, where a brand-new worried wife is pointing right back at you.

Monsters in 3 Parts

First day of vacation, Loch Ness, 1993

We glide along the choppy loch into the darkening day, me pointing out suspicious things. "Look," I say, "what's that over there? Like a large chunk of rock?"

"Rock?" he says. "Did you say 'chunk of rock'?" I point, but the monster's already gone. "Why can't you just admit that the monster is me?" he says. "Or me," I say, and laugh.

In the middle of the night, when he's deep in his dreams, there's a shadow rising shyly along the wall, and I think about how much I used to love him.

Kelp? Hell? Help?

On a smaller boat, deep into another bruised sky day, I point out sinuous shapes in the water. "Look. What's that shadow over there? A weeping puddle of kelp?"

"Puddle of hell?" he says. "Did you say 'hell'?"

I wonder why he always mishears. "Kelp," I say, *the dark, unhappy shape, the monster weeping.*

Nessie

I try to say "Nessie" when they rush me to the ER, but the name sticks inside my gullet.

"Do you remember who you were with on the boat when it capsized?" one of them asks.

"I don't think I was with anyone," I say, "nobody close anyway." Nothing I feel makes any sense to the doctors.

"The captain pulled you out," one of them says. "Can you remember the captain's face?"

Heart-shaped, wasn't it? Terribly sad?

APOCRYPHAL TALES

Skeptical scientists refuse to discuss it.

Made of satin, wasn't she? Like a shiny widow. But once she had you in her flippers, you knew: she hated her own molecules, sat on them to make them bleed. Easy to imagine her, an aging monster massaging a monster hunter with love-bubbles, perking him up where he had long been shriveled. Beads of sweat rose on the hunter's brow as his penis curled like a Fiddlehead fern.

Acclaim grew, tourists piled in, whiskey sales rose and smart men—*real scientists!*—disappeared. She craved the thrill: staged non-passion. She believed it happened nearly overnight.

So even today tourists don't dare to nap or make bluebell chains. They stay alert to see *Nessiteras Rhombopteryx* in her true form.

Long Ago Cottage Memories

I remember my husband and me in our long-ago cottage, sure that we needed to see the monster for ourselves. Or was it the fear that we had become too close to each other? Wasn't it safer to think about this monster that nobody in their right minds believed in?

Perched near the window, coffee in hand, I watch the sun sneak out of its cave. Even a finger of daylight can squash the relief out of last night's dream: my late husband dipping under the pale foam of our old sofa, squiggling safely back down to the ink-black loch, where we used to nest.

I continue to study the photos of us together, and I follow the signs. Two middle-aged dreamers, sloshing next to each other all day and night, right on this sofa, leaning and smiling and sinking — as if together, we made a kind of monster.

ONE MONSTER HUNTER'S STORY

1. "I first photographed a small, elegant creature sticking up in front, something like a silver line on the surface of the water. Through binoculars I could imagine she had a healthy, beating heart. She was wearing a hat and had strange hair. At that point I started filming.

2. Soon after the film was processed, my wife left me and married a banker, nearly 7 feet tall. I have always been only a medium-sized husband and a damaged lover, not the kind of guy a regular woman shows off to her friends. I learned not to hunt for mythical critters, unless you are ready to lose the one at home.

3. The objective, you might say, was to get a tissue sample from the fibre of the creature in the loch after I caught sight of her again. To this end I ventured forth in a small rowboat at night, dressed in a wetsuit and armed with a crossbow. When the hat came up, I'd fire a cupid's arrow into the brim and pull on the line to retrieve her smile and, after that, beat a hasty retreat. Sadly, I found nothing but inky black water, and the strange sensation that someone had been keeping me safe from harm."

KISSING THE MONSTER HUNTER

The monster hunter and I kiss so deeply that we don't see the monster. We kiss before we can see each other kissing. "Is the monster blue?" I say, kissing his lips so hard that he has to see me, has to recognize the monster in me. "One of the monsters is blue," he says, "and one of them isn't. One of them has feet, and the other one has lips." I'm laughing, we're laughing. Now we're in the same world, kissing each other so tenderly in the dream that his neck feels like a sea serpent rising from the deep. I'm on guard, but ready to be roped by the tendons in the old man's neck.

"How old am I?" I say to my monster hunter. "Old and beautiful like me," he says, "like all invisible animals are." I can feel my wrinkles reaching toward him like fishing-lines in water. Can feel the monster in him rising from the salt of my skin. Later, I'll be wringing my hands. Thoughts of capture will have taken up residence in the loch I swim in without him every day. "Help me," I say, kissing him so hard that I can finally see him.

Meeting a Hunter on the Beach

Nobody wants to know what's in there. The locals just look at it and sigh.

Meeting a Hunter on the Beach

He looked like he had just woken up from a very long nap, maybe a long lifetime nap, and had landed here on the north shore of the loch. He seemed shy. (Little known fact: monster hunters are shy.)

"What brings you out here to the hinterlands?" I asked.

"I wanted to see the loch. The water here is so deep. I love how dark that makes it look," he said, and then I realized that my face was hot. Hot face, a strange woman with a hot face. Nobody useful.

'Deep, dark', dumb things to say. My intensity. Words sunk like logs. I no longer wanted to be a floating woman, disappearing and reappearing every day.

MOON NON-MAGIC

Many scientists now believe that giant eels account for many,
if not most of the sightings.

That night Moon looked like nothing
but a piece of thrown up cheese.
Depressing.
I woke up imagining
myself stroking the monster with both hands.
Maybe Moon was in love with me,
the way my mother had loved my father—
in a possessive, sickening way.
That night I broke up with Moon to save him.
"I no longer need your flashlight
to find her," I said.

FIRST-PERSON EYE-WITNESS REPORTS: THE FACTUAL SIGHTINGS OF NESSIE

Probably the weirdest and most wonderful report of all was that made by the elderly Ms. Margarita Polkraski on June 8th, 1993. Cryptozoologist Ben Dinglefern interviewed the ailing Ms. P. and this account I regard as the most accurate:

"This was back in 1976. My on-again/off-again boyfriend Rollo and I had passed through Dores, on our way over to the Wee Drop Inn when, when just as my car was climbing a tiny knoll, an extraordinary-looking animal jerked crossed the road ahead of us, as if caught in a private moment, experiencing a series of shudders. Poor embarrassed thing, I said to Rollo, but he seemed more interested in his reflection in the rearview mirror. Rollo was finally going bald. When we were on the road together, what to do about it took up practically an entire conversation.

Rollo saw no actual skin on the monster, he said, but we were far down the road, with Rollo finger-combing his own remaining strands, before he had time to take the experience of the miraculous beast in full.

Did you see our Nessie? I asked, gasping like a star-struck child, having seen a most excellent female monster with a full, lustrous head of scales. But already she had been out of sight for a few seconds, and my Rollo was sipping from our wee flask and gasping from stress.

I can tell you right now. The creature was of a size six, and I envied her confidence in this terrible, crazy world. She had very long and thin neck, which undulated up and down, and was contorted into a series of half hoops. God, I thought, please help me find the right lover."

Remembering His Sounds of Distress

What are the food sources? Abundant with life but so dark—
what grows?

That squeezing sound when I yawn, the jaw letting me
know that it's time to march through another day. I feel like
an unknown creature in my own kitchen, making my morning
coffee, thinking that one day my hunter will return alive and
tell me that I am the only monster he's ever been looking for.
I imagine the sound of his work boots on the driveway, the
way the dog pads over to greet him. You remember me, boy?
he'd say, his words moving around as if to displace time,
talking to the new dog as if it were the old dog, thirty years
ago, talking to the new me like all that time hasn't fallen into
the loch. These days, I find myself slipping back into a deep
foamy porter, sipping it carefully in the living room, perched
on the arm of his old chair, as if sneaking up on his boat,
listening for the sound of a distressed animal in the dark.

Hump in the Mist: A Townie's Fond Memories

"If a man tells you something about himself, always believe him." —Everyone's grandmother

Me, like the loveless serpent swimming toward St Columba in the River Ness, swimming for my monster hunter on our drunken nights together. Me, pierced by the monster hunter, the hump of his problem rising out of my dreams.

But he goes, every morning, and I'm just a middle-aged townie, imagining myself next to him on the beach, where we first met, laughing about how calm the water seemed.

"You can never trust the calm," he said. But how calmly he swam into my life, his astonishing neck, the neck of a human lover.

SOUND-CLUSTERS CONSIDERED

When I heard the way sounds clustered that year, I knew that I was almost there, that the monster was nearby. And there he was in the woods—pacing, waiting.

By then I wanted to be eaten by a beautiful, freckled animal. The name no longer mattered. My life had become an overripe peach, my flesh dripping and pecked at by birds.

HUNTMYMONSTER(DOT)COM

Here the clouds are colourless,
hanging in the sky, waiting
for the right fella to call,
hungry for middle-aged fruit.
"Where do you think I live?"
I ask 20233,
the one who'd winked, despite my colorless frizz,
on huntmymonsterdotcom. Fazed not at all.
The evidence is growing, they warn us on TV.
They hunt the weary and lovesick.
And here I sit, in coffee shops, waiting!
Puttering around car boot sales,
trying on peach-coloured hats
whose shadows make my face appear sweeter.

Nessie's Story: Spotting the Monster Hunter/ Not Being Spotted

"He has soft fuzzy hair instead of quills" —*Nessiteras Rhombopteryx*

From the sea, at first, he's like a blind spot, a short, dark burst of rock. And then she sees his true form and thinks, *How unfortunate he is, with his wild hair.* This is the human who has been out to find her, who's made a whole life of it, he with his well-known face!

Hurts, she knows, not being found.

Guy from the Beach, not his name, but she feels it. A very good face, the hill of his smile...

If she could just climb up out of the sea and speak to him, this man with no net, who stands there lost to pink tufts of cloud, talking to his four-legged companion. "Let's call it a day," he says.

She fans a fin in his direction, props up her huge neck. "I'm right over here," she moans. Only the waves hear.

TRUE ROMANCE

Scientists have a dismissive attitude.

She kissed him and kissed him until he turned into a globe. She kissed the globe until it heated up. She kissed the heat until it spurted and bubbled. She kissed the crazy goop of the universe. She kissed the mess and submerged herself. She kissed him deep inside the coldest part of the loch, where they say he is protected by the world's most famous female monster.

TINY MONSTERS

Abundant with life but so dark. What grows?

In his caravan, the monster hunter keeps an aquarium filled with tiny fish. He watches them as if they are angels or bits of cork. The lint on his sweater winks at the fish, as they swim around, lukewarm, like tiny monsters waiting for an asteroid.

"How are things going?" he asks them. They sometimes glare at him because they know they will never be good enough. *Fine, just fine really,* they say silently, before they squirrel back around like smoke.

JOY TO THE MONSTER-HUNTING WORLD

After "Joy to the World" by Three Dog Night

It was joy seeing the world from his shore, eating his fish, drinking his wine. Searching for his monster. "I promise you that you're on the right path," I said. "I feel the joy, sitting here next to you on this incredible hunt."

He smiled at me as if he too felt the joy, but didn't know exactly where it lived. What if it lived with me? Like he wanted to throw away the cars and the smog and make sweet love to me. Or to the monster.

Somehow he never did either. Still, I followed him to the shore, and we looked at the ripples in the loch's deep blue water. That day, the day he almost spotted it! Oh, the joy, watching him feel it, sitting next to him on the beach, feeling like one of the creatures he loved, his rainbow rider.

I stood up and danced with his old dog, staring so hard at the loch the monster had to wake up. I remembered dancing with my best friend in her dining room, afraid of her big sisters, fairy tale monsters who told her she was ugly, who chased me out of the house just for being her friend. They laughed at her stringy hair and called me "mouse".

A grownup mouse now, dancing away from them, hunting for the real monster with a bonafide monster hunter. Finally understanding the joy in being hunted.

OBSERVATION FROM THE "RESIDENT PREDATOR"

"It looks very bad for a resident predator". —*Unnamed scientist*

My man is a bobbing cork. He wobbles like a moonstone on the beach. For nothing. His sunlit hump of night hair. Moonroof of pale-scalp skin. He is alone, and I am watching carefully. Nobody should ruin him. *Don't take a picture of him this way,* I think.

Inculcate me into your lifelong dream, man!

I peck on bubbles as if I am a prehistoric chicken. *Don't panic, Nessita-bonita,* I think.

The submarine of my body bubbles up and freezes when he stares at me and doesn't see me, stares out at this empty space within a solid object.

I sing soprano in the underwater choir. Today, effervescent. I don't love this. I don't love being this … thing.

There are sweet grasses in here. Nobody knows it. I love the dark things that wobble by. I want to tell him, *It's not all bad, this. I am not feeling the creepies, are you?* I want to say, *Don't let the sceptics win.*

BABY TEETH

"When I looked again there was nothing there."

He handed me a container filled with his baby teeth. "These are my enamels," he said. "When Mom died, I found them stuffed in her closet". I rattled the jar, and stood there thinking that his dreams were probably trapped inside there as well. Still, he dazzled me with his babyish smile, living in a caravan filled with sketches of the sea monster.

We talked around and around the real issues and it always came back to the fever he had about finding something impossible. I refused to let this go. His eyes rolled around. This was because he was trying to make me love him like a mother. Today, his lips were weirdly pink and the cavity of his mouth was a loch that a woman like me could drown in.

THE LOCH BETWEEN HER THIGHS

Loch Ness is black because the peat that washed into the loch from surrounding hills stained the water. Deep because the glaciers dug into the earth.

In the middle of the night, the monster quietly slips out from between her thighs. In sleep she must have closed her heart to it, for when she reaches out to feel it, it›s gone. She wants to cry, but it is her fault for not loving things closely enough, the sadness unearned. What will it do without her arthritic but willing body, the dark loch that lives between her thighs? A monster feels safe in there. She wonders if tacking flyers on telephone poles will make sense, *have you see this monster?* She decides it's embarrassing—her life already strange enough...She leaves the front door unlocked, gluten free crackers in the pantry—so that if the monster comes back, it will feel cared for.

She sits there wondering who to call. The night is weirdly purple, the sky a full-body bruise. Such embarrassingly red lipstick she wears, her mother would have scowled. She wears lipstick all the time, as if to protect the day from her paleness. Now, without its eyes on her, she is a damaged, less interesting creature.

She walks into the kitchen to scrounge up some supper. She

heats up a tin of soup and opens the door to the last of the terrible daylight. She can feel how much it matters— the way food feels like love, the way her mouth wants to remember what the monster tastes like.

FALSE NEUTRALITY

You sit on the floor making your face neutral.
It's okay, you say. Your thick, silvery hair
looks so much like a dog's fur.
I almost smile. *People still see it*, you say.
Not me.

I say this because I don't.
I open a beer and follow myself outside.
There is a crack in our front porch
which has been there too long,
like something deep inside
our history is trying to hatch.

There are puddles of time in those planks,
and they have begun to rot.

Blob of Understanding

"It stood erect out of the water and sailed right into our view."

There is a blob of understanding sometimes. I wake up and feel vacuumed out and clear again. Your legs, splayed over the covers as if you had had an atomic dream and it blasted you back. I look at your plaid sleeping shirt and grab my toothbrush, thinking, *Today I'll remember how to make lemon pie.* "Yowza," I say, "I've slept the whole morning away." You open one eye like a dinosaur. You smile at me with your prehistoric face.

LIVING ROOM LOCH

It's a very moody place.

The adoption of that unwanted creature, right there in the living room. His wife watching telly, drinking wine, not looking at the monster swimming around. The animal gazing into his eyes, finding him interesting and rare.

Later, he makes a list of things he cannot do to please her. Increasingly he falls asleep in the water, next to the animal. Its sharp nose against his throat; its wet, dark breath becoming his own.

Unusual Loch Observations

Professor Boyd is known as the man who killed off the Loch Ness monster by exposing the fraud. But now he says he believed in the monster.

Dinosaur to Dinosaur

You probably weren't expecting a dinosaur, I said to the monster hunter. *I don't even know how to use a dating app,* he replied. His skin appeared non water-soluble, but my heart was a silly old sponge. Our lips stretched toward each other like fishing lines.

Way Up North

I found a mottled old fisherman who might sort of love me. He was staring out at the loch for some sign that his monster was safe. He threw me a rope made of waterlogged compliments, then dove back into the water to save her.

Martyr

He waded into the loch, wetsuit shining like a renegade seal in the mist. Nessie, they say, lived to end his happiness. If he walked his dog twenty minutes late in the morning, her prehistoric eyes became overfilled buckets.

UNCORKED

Whatever he said next would unpop the cork in my behavior which was going all eyebrows up. Because I was bait. Because he was neon happy around invisible creatures, and the more impossible the animal, the easier it felt to paddle near him.

INJURED MONSTER

When I brought the monster home, Mom flashed her pearly-yellow teeth and lipstick-stained smile. *You're juicier than the last,* she said, pinching his bottom. She hooked him her flipper, kissed the beast on his snout. *This one is injured, Ma,* I reminded her.

HERE WE ARE, UNTIL WE FEEL THIS USELESS

"I just couldn't believe it. It was quite big and emerald green. I couldn't even an exact size on it — other than she was freakin' gorgeous." —John Stewart, 1984

So much about getting old is being ready to see the monster who shambles to your door with a cigarette dangling from her beautiful mouth, a satisfied gleam in her eyes, as if the world has finally made love to her the right way. But today I am all fished out, back to square one with the stars, drinking alone and hoping for a dreamy slumber.

A Monster Hunter's Long Suffering Wife (or a Make-Believe Wife, Long-Suffering)

The wife looks inside the doorway of my mind and says, *Are you ever going to tell it straight?*

I turn on the music in my head and wonder. The sun shines like a blood bubble through the window. It has an orange halo, so I follow it outside to my boat. Today, the loch is crusted over with memories from a distant shore.

WHAT HE DIDN'T FIND AND WHAT HE DID

The scientific community explains alleged sightings of the Loch Ness Monster as hoaxes, wishful thinking, dreaming, and the misidentification of mundane objects

He did not find the monster, but he found a way to tell people what he didn't find. He called it "full disclosure". His sign read, "WE PROBABLY DON'T HAVE A MONSTER." It made him less accountable for miracles. He was in love again and wanted everything out on the table before she arrived. She may not look ready, and he'd forgive her for that. Her name was Salina. He met her on a website for recovered dreamers who wanted to get married quickly, before the next dream. He liked what she stood for. She said, *"No Hollywood happy-ending for Salina* is just fine." He liked that. He liked that just fine.

MEMORIES OF A KISS

Almost every sizeable body of water has a hunter associated with it...

Last time I was at this place, an old monster hunter tried to kiss me. We'd had a nice discussion and ended up strolling around the loch. It was a lovely day, and the hedgehogs were out. When he leaned me against a thick tree trunk, I felt a bit pleased to know that this was not in any way going to be just a normal day. I was going to be caught. Some old hunters are like this, I now understand, unable to stop. I've read the handbook on this! So now I sit on the beach very close to him, wary of young men, holding my old dog close, tasting the salt from each wave, while the world's oldest monster hunter lets me know why it took him so long to find me.

How Stuckness Changes Things

Wakes have been reported when the loch is calm, with no boats nearby.

I knew that he was mostly blind to what it felt like to be any person besides himself. He blurred the city by ignoring it, driving through it like a fly stuck in the closet, driving as far north as he could. I could tell he had lost his sense of amazement and didn't know why he was sad. The new landscape was unfamiliar. But now we were on the other side of the hills, away from old friends with their luck and their money, so many terrible traps. Instead of a beach, a deserted cove, shaped like a cake bowl before the batter runs.

MY HUSBAND THE MOUNTAIN

After 1983 the search ... (for the) possibility that there just might be continues to enthrall a small number for whom eye-witness evidence outweighs all other considerations.

My husband was a mountain, trees low, weedy paths.

Frost on his lips when he went outside.

There was a sea monster who loved him before me, spoiled him.

She liked to set up tents, star gaze, flowers in her hair.

Awake all night, compass in hand.

The day he left this world he asked me. Where had she gone?

Who cares? I answered.

She loved invisibility, he said. *Yes, indeed!* I said.

I hated her salty skin, slimy dreams.

The night I finally asked, his face shaded over.

How did it feel to make love with her?

She would take me in her arms, he said.

Sift me through her fingers.

Frost on his lips when he went outside.

THE ANIMAL

"There's something here that we don't understand, and there's something here that's larger than a fish, maybe some species that hasn't been detected before. I don't know."

The boy wakes up and knows exactly where his creature is. They are eating dinner together again, like in his dream. The father will be home but invisible, adept with his "disappearing act". The mother will be talking to her therapist on the phone. The boy knows the creature so deeply that he can feel its calloused hand-skin. At dinner, the creature might be talking with him about their mother's hair color, her survivor tattoo. It might speak directly to the father about things. "Hey there, your wife is looking sparkly!" Very casual. Anyone could see how the father doesn't look at the mother anymore. Not into her eyes, anyway. The creature will steer the father back to where things started, when the family was still a family.

Won't You Come Out to Play?

"....so I think we can be fairly sure that there is probably not a giant scaly reptile swimming around in Loch Ness," he said.

Tonight the dark is a threat, knowing she loves morning like he does. Knowing she loves driftwood, and families of displaced ducks. The bruise of sky and the wind and the night birds suck. Like him, she hates the low sound of the wind and he hopes it will stop. "Nessita," he says. She took him to the other side of the loch, and in his mind, they were beautiful together. She came out to play only once, back in 1993, because he asked her to. He can still hear her laughing, even in the dark.

ACKNOWLEDGMENTS

Grateful acknowledgment is made to the following publications in which these stories (or earlier versions of these stories) originally appeared:

SurVision:

"Meeting a Hunter on the Beach"

"Moon Non-Magic"

Ghost Parachute:

"Kissing the Monster Hunter"

Ink, Sweat & Tears:

"Living Room Loch"

South Florida Poetry Journal:

"What He Didn't Find, and What He Did"

"Unusual Loch Observations"

"Here we are, until we feel this useless"

"Memories of a Kiss"

About the Author

MEG POKRASS is the award-winning author of 8 flash fiction collections and 2 flash novellas, including *Spinning to Mars* (Blue Light Book Award, 2021) and *The Loss Detector* (Bamboo Dart Press, 2020). Her work has appeared in over 900 literary journals has been anthologized in 3 Norton anthologies: *Flash Fiction International* (W.W. Norton, 2015), *New Micro: Exceptionally Short Fiction* (W.W. Norton, 2018), and *Flash Fiction America* (W. W. Norton & Co., 2023). She is the Series Co-Editor of *Best Microfiction* and Founding Editor of *New Flash Fiction Review*. Meg lives in Inverness Scotland.

http://www.megpokrass.com

112 N. Harvard Ave. #65
Claremont, CA 91711

chapbooks@bamboodartpress.com

www.bamboodartpress.com

www.ingramcontent.com/pod-product-compliance
Lightning Source LLC
Chambersburg PA
CBHW080756120626
46557CB00006B/1292